M.H. - For Sebastian and his Uncle Jim; two (Thunder)birds of a feather.

D.T. - For all my girls with love; Nancy, Maddy, and Lils

...and a special thanks to Amy for her help in making this book a reality.

Edsel McFarlan's
NEW CAR

Written by Max Holechek   Illustrated by Darrell Toland

Published by
Book Publishers Network
P. O. Box 2256
Bothell, WA 98041
425 483-3040
www.bookpublishersnetwork.com

ISBN 10: 1-935359-40-1   ISBN 13: 978-1-935359-40-1
LCCN: 2009939052

Holechek, Max.

Edsel McFarlan's new car / written by Max Holechek ; illustrated by
Darrell Toland. -- 1st ed. -- Bothell, WA : Book Publishers Network,
c2010.

p. : ill. ; cm.

ISBN: 978-1-935539-40-1
Audience: Ages 4-8.
Summary: When a young car enthusiast receives a plastic
model kit to match the true scale of his passion, his entire
neighborhood buckles-up for a wild ride.

1. Automobiles--Juvenile fiction. 2. Automobiles--Models--
Juvenile fiction. 3. Models and modelmaking--Juvenile fiction.
4. Boys--Juvenile fiction. 5. Hobbies--Juvenile fiction. 6. [Cars--
Fiction. 7. Cars--Models--Fiction. 8. Models and modelmaking--
Fiction. 9. Boys--Fiction. 10. Hobbies--Fiction.] I. Toland, Darrell.
II. Title.

PZ7.H7073 E37 2010   2009939052
[E]   1006

Printed in the United States
10 9 8 7 6 5 4 3 2 1

Special thanks to Speed Racer Enterprises for permisson to use the
Speed Racer image.

Please wipe your shoes before entering this book.
www.edselmcfarlan.com

Edsel McFarlan loved cars.

His neighbors called it
"an obsession."

On Tuesday evening, Edsel saw the ad.

On Saturday morning,
the box arrived.

Edsel McFarlan loved his new model.

His neighbors called it "peculiar."

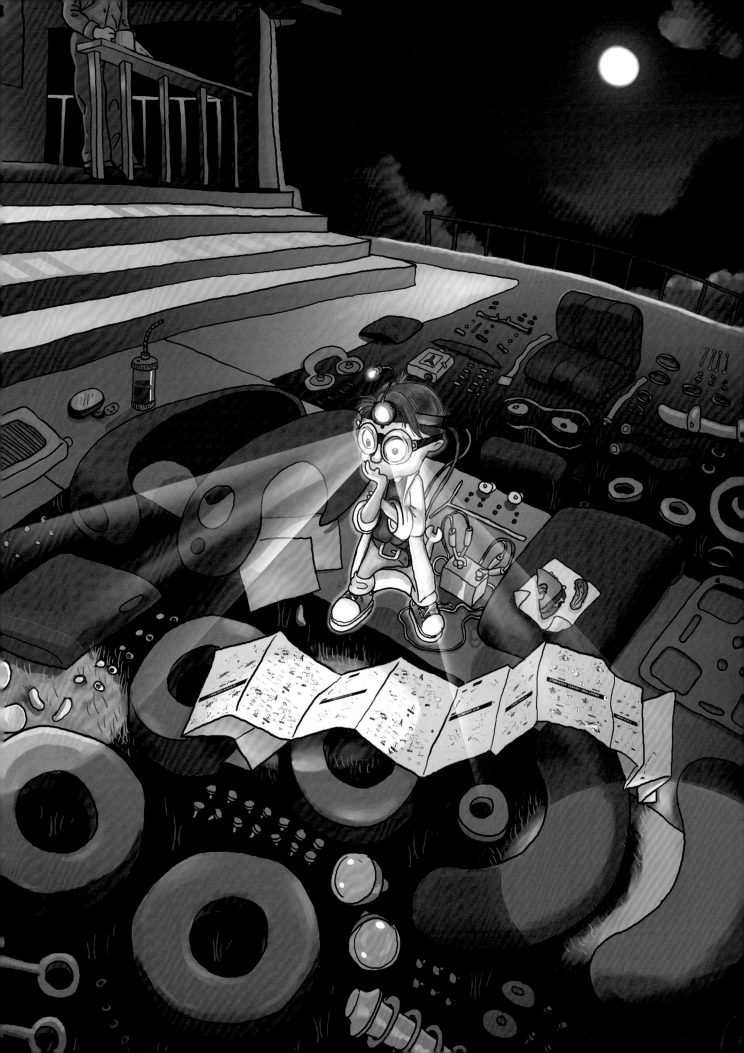

On Sunday afternoon,
the car was nearly finished.

The model had many
realistic features.

For instance, the wheels spun freely.

The steering wheel turned the front tires.

It had shiny chrome hubcaps and a bumper.

The doors could open.

Under the hood was a highly detailed engine.

It had molded front seats.

Edsel McFarlan loved his new car.

His neighbors called it
"a lemon."

Perhaps they were right.

Much Later.

Edsel McFarlan
used to love cars.

His neighbors called it
"a phase."